# Our Classroom

## by Larry Hutton
## illustrated by Patrick Girouard

HOUGHTON MIFFLIN     BOSTON

We listen to our teacher.

We talk in soft voices
when others are working.

We listen to our friends
read their stories.

We share the materials
with each other.

We help each other
and work together.

We follow the rules
on the playground.

We like to work and play
together in our classroom.